ALEXIS SHEPPARD

ALEXIS SHEPPARD

CHRISTOPHER TRAVAIL GATES

ARPress

ARPress LLC
45 Dan Road Suite 5
Canton MA 02021
Hotline: 1(888) 821-0229
Fax: 1(508) 545-7580

Ordering Information:
Quantity sales. Special discounts are available on quantity purchases by corporations, associations, and others. For details, contact the publisher at the address above.

Printed in the United States of America.

ISBN-13:   Softcover   979-8-89330-982-9
            eBook   979-8-89330-983-6

Library of Congress Control Number: 2024902687

About the Author

Christopher Travail Gates grew up in rural Georgia in the small quaint town of Woodbury. It's about an hour outside of Atlanta. He began his love for writing at an early age. He's the oldest of two children. Christopher has always had talents in reading, writing, drawing, and sports. His adventure for knowledge and his inquisitiveness structure his upbringing. He's an avid sportsman with a love of basketball, football, baseball, and track and field. His first publication brings his imagination into focus, guiding his reader through a world of infinite possibilities.

It's a typical Monday morning for sixteen-year-old Alexis Sheppard. The alarm sounds on her cell phone; she stumbles out of bed and gets ready for school. Once dressed, Alexis heads downstairs to have breakfast with her parents.

As she walks into the kitchen, she sees her mother, Catherine, and her father, Alvin, attentively watching a breaking story on the morning news. Catherine Sheppard is a criminal defense attorney in Atlanta, Georgia. She is well known for her fiery nature as she represents her clients in and outside of the courtroom. Alvin Sheppard is a Zone 1 detective for Atlanta's Police Department. With twenty years of experience, Alvin is said to be one of the most inspiring police detectives serving the city of Atlanta. He is an inspiration to Alexis most of all. She is fascinated by her father's profession and plans to follow in his footsteps one day. In fact, after graduating from high school, she plans to attend college and major in criminal justice before joining the police academy.

"What's going on?" Alexis asks. Her father quickly turns off the television.

"Nothing," he responds, "just another day in Atlanta."

Alexis is an only child, and her parents are very protective, especially Alvin. He tries to shield Alexis from learning the dangers of the city and his work, but she is always asking about the crimes and cases broadcast on the news. He is strongly against her dreams of following in his footsteps but ultimately knows he can't stop her.

"The two of you should have another child. I would love to share this overprotective-parent experience with a little brother or sister," Alexis says sarcastically.

"One Sheppard child is more than enough," her mother says.

As the Sheppard family sits down for breakfast, Alvin asks Alexis if she is excited about taking martial arts classes. Alexis says yes, she is looking forward to it. Maria and Sandy, Alexis's best friends, are taking the classes as well.

"I feel more comfortable knowing I won't be taking the classes alone, and will have Maria and Sandy with me," Alexis says.

"That's good," Catherine says.

"Yes, I'm glad you are taking those classes, Alexis. You will be able to defend yourself when I am not around," Alvin says.

Alexis snickers at her dad and says, "I know, Dad, I know."

As Catherine places a pitcher of orange juice on the table, she hands Alexis an informational booklet for the University of Georgia.

"So, Alexis, have you made a decision on the college or university you're attending in the fall?" Catherine asks. Catherine has been trying to persuade Alexis to attend the University of Georgia since her freshman year in high school, but Alexis, as always, has a different plan. Alexis looks at her parents. Her mother is sitting at the edge of her seat, and her father sits with a smirk on his face. Alvin knows Catherine is not going to like Alexis's answer.

"Well, I narrowed it down to three—Harvard, Georgetown, and Howard University," Alexis says. Catherine sits in silence for a moment, wondering if her hearing is impaired since she didn't hear Alexis say University of Georgia.

"All of those are excellent choices, but you're not going to consider my alma mater, the University of Georgia at all?" Catherine asks. Before Alexis can respond, her father jumps in.

"Alexis, at least consider your mother's alma mater. It will keep you in the state and close to home," Alvin says, winking at Alexis.

"Mom, the University of Georgia is a great school, but I want to go down my own path," Alexis says. Catherine looks at her daughter.

Alexis reminds her of herself when she was that age, wanting to be and do her own thing. Catherine agrees with Alexis and decides not to pressure her on choosing the University of Georgia.

"Do you know where Maria and Sandy are going in the Fall?" Catherine asks.

"I think Maria is considering Emory. She wants to be a nurse. Sandy is going to Georgia State University. She hasn't decided on a major yet," Alexis explains.

Suddenly, Alvin's cell phone rings. It is the chief of police. Alvin must leave for work immediately. Alexis wonders if it has anything to do with the breaking news story her parents were watching on the television earlier.

"No time for breakfast," Alvin says.

"I'm off to serve and protect." He kisses his daughter and wife goodbye and heads out the door.

Alexis finishes her breakfast shortly after her father leaves. She gathers her things, hugs her mom goodbye, and hurries out the door. She has to make it to the bus stop on time. If she is not there before Ms. Johnson, the bus driver, she will have to walk to school. Ms. Johnson waits for no one.

Once Alexis arrives at school, she meets Maria Hernandez and Sandy Martin on the front steps. Maria is fussy because she forgot to study for another one of Mr. Campbell's test. She paces back and forth, trying to think of an excuse to give Mr. Campbell. Maria never studies for a test. Instead, she is always on her phone, taking selfies or strolling through various social media applications. Sandy nonchalantly watches Maria have her moment. She's the quietest out of the three but knows how to have a good time. Alexis looks at Sandy, and the two start to laugh.

After Maria finally calms down and accepts her fate, the three friends head into the school building to start their day. The bell for first period rings, and Alexis heads toward Mr. Campbell's class. Maria tries to dawdle at her locker, but Alexis wraps her arm around Maria's and pulls her along.

"Let's go, Maria," Alexis says. Sandy chuckles at her two friends and tells them she will see them later at lunch.

Alexis and Maria reach Mr. Campbell's classroom just before the tardy bell rings. Mr. Campbell is standing at the door.

"Good morning, Miss Hernandez. I hope you're ready for the test this morning," Mr. Campbell says tauntingly. Maria rolls her eyes and walks to her seat. Alexis tries to walk in behind Maria but is stopped by Mr. Campbell.

"Alexis, Principal Payne has requested your presence in her office," Alexis looks at Mr. Campbell, surprised.

"Why?" asks Alexis.

"I don't know why, but I hope one of my brightest students is not in trouble," Mr. Campbell says. He hurries Alexis along and closes his classroom door.

All the way to Principal Payne's office, Alexis ponders different reasons why she is being asked there. She's never been called to the office before. It is strange.

"Good morning," Alexis says as she walks through the office door. In synchrony, everyone greets Alexis with a friendly good morning and a smile. Alexis knows something is up now.

The office staff isn't very friendly with students, not even honor students like her. Principal Payne walks out of her office. Alexis tries to read her face but cannot. Principal Payne is stoic. No one can tell what she is thinking or feeling ever.

"Come into my office, Alexis," Principal Payne says. Alexis walks into Principal Payne's office and stands in front of her desk. As Principal Payne walks in, she closes the door behind her.

"Have a seat, Alexis," Principal Payne directs. As Alexis sits down, she sees Principal Payne pulling up a chair beside her. Staring into Alexis's eyes, she says,

"I received a phone call from your mother shortly after you arrived today. She is on her way to release you from school early. Your father has suffered an injury and is being transported to the hospital."

Alexis's body starts to numb. Before she can say anything, she sees her mother, Catherine, and her Uncle James Sherman walking into the office. As her eyes swell with tears, Alexis runs out of Principal Payne's office and into her mother's arms. While Alexis is being comforted by her mother, her Uncle Sherman signs Alexis's early release forms. Once he finishes, they all head out the door. As they walk up to the police cruiser, Alexis notices fresh bruises on Uncle Sherman's face and hands.

"Uncle Sherman, were you with my dad when he was injured?" questions Alexis.

"Yes, but I will explain everything once we get going," replies Uncle Sherman.

Uncle Sherman, or James Sherman, is Alvin's partner on the police force. Alvin and James have been partners for almost fifteen years. Their families are very close. Holidays, vacations, and leisure times are always spent with one another. Before Alexis can ask Uncle Sherman again about her father, he begins to tell of the events that led up to his hospitalization.

"Before Al arrived to pick me up, I received a phone call from an informant. He told me one of the local drug dealers we've been keeping an eye on was on the move. He and his crew caught wind of the drug bust the force was planning for today," Sherman says.

"Once Al got there, I told him we had to move right away," Sherman continues.

"So, we did just that. We got there, and Al went in first. I was behind him, covering his back, or at least I thought I was." Sherman's voice starts to crackle. He takes a deep breath and continues.

"Somehow, I ended up separated from Al, then all of a sudden, I heard gunshots. I ran toward where I heard the shots being fired. That's when I saw him, my partner, my friend, lying face down on the ground with multiple gunshot wounds."

Catherine interrupts and says, "Did you see anyone else, any suspects, witnesses?"

"No," Sherman says, "no one was around."

"What happened next?" Alexis asks anxiously.

"I called 911 and then your mother. As soon as the first responders arrived, I headed over to get her." Sherman finishes the tragic tale of events as they arrive at the hospital. At the hospital, Catherine rushes straight to the nurse's station, asking for the whereabouts of her husband, Alvin Sheppard. Alexis is right behind her.

"Excuse me, nurse, can you please tell me where I can find Alvin Sheppard?" Catherine asks frantically. The ER doctor assigned to Alvin is standing in the hallway, waiting for their arrival. He walks over to the nurse's station where Catherine and Alexis wait impatiently for information about Alvin.

"Mrs. Catherine Sheppard?"

"Yes," Catherine responds.

"Alvin Sheppard's wife and next of kin?" the doctor asks.

Alexis interjects, "There's no time for formal greetings. Where is my father, how is he, can we see him?" asks Alexis demandingly.

Sherman grabs hold of Alexis and pulls her into one of the private waiting rooms.

"Mrs. Sheppard, I am the doctor who was assigned to your husband upon his arrival at the ER today. Unfortunately, I have some grave news."

The doctor pulls Catherine further to the side and explains that Alvin arrived at the hospital's ER unresponsive. His injuries are severe, and there is nothing that they can do but make him comfortable. The hospital has placed Alvin in a medically induced coma, but the only thing keeping him alive are the life support systems. The doctor asks Catherine to consider taking him off of life support. Although Alexis and Sherman are sitting in a private waiting room, they heard everything the doctor told Catherine.

Alexis collapses to the floor in tears. Sherman picks up Alexis and tries to comfort her. Still heavy with emotions, she walks to her mother who is still standing outside with the doctor. Catherine asks if she can see Alvin. The doctor agrees. The doctor leads the three into Alvin's room. Catherine and Alexis slowly walk into the room first. Sherman pulls up a chair near Alvin for Catherine to sit in. Alexis stands beside her mother. Catherine takes hold of Alvin's hand and begins to sob.

"What am I going to do without you? I can't lose you," Catherine says.

"Daddy, you're a fighter. I know you're in there somewhere," Alexis says.

"Mommy, you can't take him off of life support."

Sherman interrupts, "Catherine, the doctor said there is nothing they can do for Alvin. We both know Alvin would not want to suffer. I think that you should really consider not just your feelings or Alexis's feelings but Alvin's."

"He's a fighter," Alexis says angrily to Sherman.

"I know he's a fighter, but unfortunately, this is a fight he cannot win. Let's do the right thing. Let's do what's right for Alvin. Let him rest in peace," Sherman says as he places his hand on Catherine's shoulder.

Catherine sits for a moment in silence. As she starts to sob again, she nods in agreement with Sherman. Sherman hurries out to get the doctor. Catherine signs the paperwork to take her husband, Alvin, off of life support. The doctor tells Catherine that she can go home. The hospital will call once all life support systems are removed and Alvin is pronounced dead.

"We will call you at the time of his death," the doctor says. But Catherine declines.

She says, "I want to be with him until his final breath." After the last machine is turned off, Alvin lives for forty-five minutes, then surrounded by his loved ones—his wife, Catherine, his daughter, Alexis, and his partner and friend, James Sherman— Alvin Sheppard dies.

Four days later, Alvin Sheppard is laid to rest. Chief of Police Booker delivers the eulogy.

"To serve and protect is a phrase written within our policeman's oath. It is the phrase Detective Alvin Sheppard always declared before heading off into the field. For twenty-five years, Alvin committed himself to this oath of serving and protecting others. He was an amazing detective. I was looking forward to one day, naming him the new chief of police. Today, we grieve a terrible lost. Tomorrow, though our hearts may still be heavy, we will continue to serve and protect the city of Atlanta, in the name of Alvin Sheppard. He will truly be missed."

After the funeral, Alexis withdraws from everyone—her mom, Uncle Sherman, Maria, and Sandy. She stays shut up in her room.

Several months later, Alexis graduates from high school with honors. She attends Harvard University, majoring in psychology with a concentration in forensic psychology. Consumed with grief since her father's death, Alexis is determined to not only solve his murder but understand why he was murdered in the first place.

Four years later, Alexis graduates from college with honors. She returns home to Atlanta two years later, after completing her master's program, bound to her goal of solving her father's murder. Alexis moves back into her childhood home with her mother, Catherine. Her plan is to build up her savings in order to find a nice place of her own. Catherine's heart is full. She is extremely happy to have her daughter back home. To celebrate Alexis's graduation and her return home, Catherine cooks Alexis's favorite meal, spaghetti and meatballs. It does not take long for Alexis to find a job. In fact, the first day of her job search ends once she walks into her father's old police precinct. Sherman, her father's former partner and friend, is the newly elected chief of police. He interviews Alexis right there on the spot.

"Why do you want to be a cop?" Sherman asks Alexis.

"I want to make a difference in the city of Atlanta," Alexis begins.

"I also want to solve my father's murder. I know someone is responsible for his death, and I have to find out who. I need closure but can't have closure until I find out who did it and put them behind bars." Chief Sherman, although hesitant, hires Alexis and quickly moves her through the precinct's orientation process.

"I will have you a partner at the end of the week. Until then, you're on desk duty," Chief Sherman says.

Alexis doesn't mind being placed on desk duty. She sees it as the perfect opportunity to review her father's case files.

"Chief, since I have desk duty, do you mind if I take a look at my father's case files?" Alexis inquires. Chief Sherman is reluctant but gives her the go-ahead.

"Yes, you can take a look. If you find something, let me know," Chief Sherman says.

Alexis walks down to the basement of the precinct where the records are kept. It's not long before she finds her father's case files, but she also searches for another file, an arrest record to be exact, the arrest record of Jesus Montoya, aka Death King.

The only information Alexis already has on Montoya is he was arrested for the murder of her father but was acquitted. At a desk, Alexis sits and combs through Montoya's record. He has a long list of arrests and charges, many made by her dad and Sherman. Alexis wonders why he is not in jail. She finds an address for Montoya and decides to pay him a visit later. She wants to focus on new leads. After searching through the files for a while, Alexis finds the name and address of Mario Espinoza. Mario was with Montoya on serval occasions when he was arrested. She believes he is a good candidate for questioning.

She finds his address and decides to talk to him before she goes off duty. Knowing she isn't supposed to leave the precinct, especially with her partner being absent, Alexis sneaks away without Chief Sherman knowing, to question Mario.

Alexis reaches Mario's house. She takes a deep breath and heads toward the front door. As Alexis steps onto the porch, she sees someone peering out of the curtains. She rings the doorbell, but Mario isn't the one who opens the door. It's her longtime friend, Maria.

"Well, look who it is," Maria says as she stands in the doorway. Alexis is surprised to see her longtime friend Maria standing there.

"Maria," Alexis says, startled.

Alexis never thought she would see Maria again. She stopped talking to her and Sandy after her father's death, with no ill intentions, but knew she was hurting her best friends' feelings, especially Maria's. Maria often tried to call and reach out to Alexis, but Alexis never responded. Alexis thinks of apologizing to Maria and explaining to her that she wanted to reach out but couldn't before asking for Mario. Before Alexis can open her mouth, Maria asks why Alexis is there.

"Why are you here at my house, Alexis?" Maria asks.

"I'm looking for a man by the name of Mario Espinoza. Do you know him and/or his whereabouts?" Alexis asks.

Maria knows exactly who Mario is. He is her boyfriend, and they live together in the house Alexis has paid a visit to. Alexis questions Maria about whether or not she knows Mario is a former drug dealer and still hangs out with other drug dealers.

"Yes, I know Mario and all about his past life," Maria says.

"He's changed." Maria sizes Alexis up and down, looking at her in her police uniform.

"I see you've followed in your father's footsteps. I can't believe it. You could have been anything, and you chose to be a police officer," Maria says.

Alexis abruptly interjects Maria.

"I'm here to see Mario. Is he home?" she says.

Maria tells Alexis Mario isn't there, so Alexis hands Maria one of her cards. She tells Maria to call her if she hears from Mario or when he returns home. As Maria closes the door, Alexis sees a shadow moving swiftly in the back of the house. It is Mario running away.

"Stop! Stop!" Alexis yells. A chase between Alexis, Mario, and Maria begins. It does not last long. It ends after Mario runs out into the street and gets hit by a car.

Alexis pins Mario down and asks, "Do you know who killed my father?"

Mario shouts in pain, "What are you talking about? Call an ambulance!" Alexis, however, interrogates him further.

"I know you killed my father or know who did! Tell me," Alexis demands.

In pain, Mario says, "I don't know. I promise. Please call an ambulance for help." Maria finally catches up to Alexis and Mario.

She kneels down at Mario's side, then looks up at Alexis.

"What's wrong with you?" Maria angrily screams.

Alexis tells Maria that Mario knows something about her father's death. Maria, angrier than before, screams, "He doesn't know anything about your father's death. He's changed his life around for the better."

Maria continues to tell Alexis that they were once best friends and if she knew anything or anybody that may have information about her dad's death, she would tell her. Alexis looks at Maria and Mario remorsefully and says, "I'm sorry, but please, if you hear anything, let me know." She looks directly at Mario and apologizes to him. Mario says he understood Alexis's motivations. His father was murdered too and knows how Alexis feels. Mario says, "I will let you know if I remember anything."

Feeling a little ashamed and defeated, Alexis heads back to the precinct. She walks in and sees Chief Sherman standing at her desk, waiting for her. He doesn't look happy at all. In fact, he's not happy. He has heard about Alexis's chase and Mario's car incident.

"Where have you been?" Sherman asks.

"I went to go question a suspect in my dad's case. I'm sorry, but I thought he was the guy," Alexis responds.

"You went to go question a suspect without backup," Sherman exclaims.

"Without my okay, you leave the precinct, alone, to question a possible murder suspect. I told you, Alexis, if you find anything to let me know." Chief Sherman takes a deep breath and continues,

"Alexis, after your father's death, I vowed to always look out for you. You know better than to go out on your own." Alexis apologizes and says it won't happen again. Sherman tells her it better not and heads back into his office.

Disappointed about the recent events, Alexis is happy to see her shift is coming to an end. She heads to the lockers and changes into her civilian clothes. She is meeting another longtime friend, Sandy, after work. The night before, Catherine tells her Sandy's mother recently died of cancer. She suggested Alexis reach out to Sandy, and she did. The two agreed to meet the next day. Alexis is nervous, wondering if her reunion with Sandy will be just as unpleasant as Maria's. After her lunch with Sandy, Alexis plans to visit Montoya at the address she found in his arrest records earlier.

Alexis arrives five minutes late to meet with Sandy. As she walks into the restaurant, she sees Sandy already sitting at a table. It's not long before Sandy sees Alexis walking up. Sandy gets up to greet Alexis. The once talkative friends stand for a moment in awkward silence. Finally, Sandy gestures for Alexis to sit and join her at the table. Taking a deep breath, Alexis begins the conversation with condolences on the death of Sandy's mother.

"I'm sorry to hear about your mom," Alexis says. Sandy nods her head and utters a soft thank-you. Alexis gazes upon Sandy's face, noticing how much her looks resemble her mother.

To build the conversation, Alexis starts reminiscing the bright and bubbly days of their friendship.

A smile emerges on Alexis's face, and she lightly chuckles. Sandy starts mirroring Alexis. For Sandy, smiles and laughter are highly contagious.

"What are we smiling about?" Sandy asks.

"I was just thinking about our high school days and how much fun we had together," Alexis says.

"Especially the days your mom carpooled." Sandy begins to laugh harder.

"Yes, she would take us all over Atlanta," Sandy says.

With the ice broken, Alexis and Sandy spend the afternoon laughing and catching up. As her lunch date with Sandy comes to an end, Alexis regretfully thinks about how she lost contact with Sandy and also Maria. Before leaving, she self-consciously pressures herself to mentioning her thoughts to Sandy.

"Sandy," Alexis begins.

"I'm sorry. I pushed you and Maria away after my father's murder. I should have stayed in contact." Sandy tries to interrupt Alexis, but Alexis tells her she needs to speak her truth.

Alexis continues, "Moving back home, I've realized not only did I lose my father, but I also lost my best friends." Alexis ends with the wipe of a fallen tear from her face.

Sandy grabs Alexis's hand.

"People grieve in different ways, and as your friend, I knew and understood you wanted to grieve alone," Sandy says.

"You didn't lose a friend in me. I'm glad you reached out to me, and I hope we can do this again soon." Sandy ends the conversation with open arms, welcoming a hug.

Alexis leaves the restaurant lighthearted, knowing she still has Sandy as a friend, but the feeling is short-lived as she heads off to meet Jesus Montoya. It's not long before Alexis reaches the address listed in Montoya's records. It's an old, abandoned building owned by Jesus Montoya. It's also the very building where her father was murdered six years ago. There are a couple of call girls hanging outside the building. Solicitation is just one of the many arrests Montoya's records listed. Alexis gets out of the car and heads over to the girls.

"Excuse me," Alexis says.

"Does anyone know where I can find Jesus Montoya?" she asks. No one answers Alexis. In fact, they pretend as if she isn't even there.

"Does anyone know where the Death King is?" Alexis asks again.

This time, the girls, still ignoring her begin to walk away. Alexis rolls her eyes and yells Thank you! to the two young women and then heads back to the car.

Back inside her car, Alexis puts her head down on the steering wheel. She knew the task of solving her father's murder isn't going to be easy, but she didn't think it is going to be this hard either. All of a sudden, Alexis's phone rings. It's Mario.

"I have a name for you," Mario says.

"Have you heard the name Jesus Montoya or Death King?"

Alexis's heart begins to race.

"Yes, I know the name. I was just looking for him. Do you know where he is now?" Alexis asks.

Mario tells Alexis he owns a popular night lounge in Atlanta called After Six and that he's there around this time every day until closing. Alexis is thankful for Mario's call. She types the address of the night lounge into her GPS and heads to see Jesus Montoya, the Death King.

Alexis arrives at the After Six lounge forty-five minutes later. As she walks up to the entrance, the security guard greets her.

"How can I help you lady?" the security guard asks.

"I'm here to see Jesus," Alexis says flirtingly, trying to make sure she gets in. Suspicious, the security guard asks Alexis why she wants to meet with Montoya. Alexis lies, saying she's looking for a bartending job. He looks Alexis up and down, and even asks her to turn around.

Finally, he says "follow me" and takes Alexis to Montoya's table. Alexis sits down at the table and starts to introduce herself, but Montoya already knows who she is.

"What can I do for you, Miss Sheppard?" Montoya asks smirkingly

"I'm here to ask you questions about a murder that happened approximately six years ago. An officer was murdered. His name was Alvin Sheppard," Alexis says.

Montoya puts his hand up signaling Alexis to stop speaking.

"I don't know anything about a murder," Montoya says.

Alexis doesn't believe him and continues to question Montoya further.

"You were arrested and charged…"

"And acquitted," Montoya interrupts.

"I was arrested, charged, and acquitted, but continue," he says arrogantly.

Alexis continues, "You were charged and arrested for the murder of Alvin Sheppard. In his case files, your name is mentioned several times. The building where the murder took place is in fact owned by you…"

"I did not kill your father," Montoya interrupts Alexis again.

"But you know who did?" Montoya starts to smirk. He knows he has Alexis's full attention.

Montoya leans forward and says, "If I tell you what I know, what's in it for me?" Desperate for answers, Alexis tries to think of what would be most appealing to Montoya. She tells him he will not face any jail time, if what he says is true, and that she can offer protection from the person responsible for her father's murder.

Montoya and his bodyguard start laughing.

"I don't need your protection, Alexis. I have enough policía on my payroll," Montoya says with a wink.

Alexis stares across the table at Montoya, processing his words and actions. She thinks to herself, who on the police force is a part of his payroll and why he winked at her.

"Was my father a part of your payroll," Alexis asks.

"No," Montoya says with a smile.

"From what I heard, your dad was actually one of the good guys, but his partner…that's another story." Alexis stands up and says,

"You're telling me my father's partner, James Sherman, now Police Chief Sherman works for you?" Montoya, still seated, signals his bodyguard over to the table to escort Alexis out.

Before the bodyguard removes Alexis, Montoya says to her,

"I've said too much. However, I'll give you some advice before you go. Don't trust Chief Sherman. He's not what he seems to be and never was."

Alexis is escorted out of the club by Montoya's bodyguard. He watches Alexis until she gets in her car and drives away. Alexis drives all the way home, dismayed about all she has learned from Montoya.

At home, Alexis walks in and sees her mother, Catherine, sitting on the sofa watching TV. She sits down by her mother almost in tears. Catherine asks Alexis,

"What is wrong?" Alexis tells her she thinks Uncle Sherman may be involved in the murder of her father.

"That's impossible," Catherine says.

"I can't believe you would think that about your Uncle Sherman. He has been there for us since your father's death. He just hired you to work on the force under him," Catherine says.

Alexis tells the details of the events that led her to believe James Sherman is a possible suspect in the murder of Alvin Sheppard.

"I think Uncle Sherman is on this drug dealer's payroll. His name is Jesus Montoya. Have you heard of him?" Alexis says. Catherine has heard the name before, at the law office and in conversations she shared with Alvin from time to time but did not have in-depth knowledge.

"I know about some prior arrests your father and James completed," Catherine answers. Alexis continues asking her mother to think back to conversations she had with her father.

"Looking at his arrest records, I noticed each time he was arrested, he got off. Why?" asks Alexis.

"Why was he able to get off each time he was arrested? Did Dad tell you?" Catherine tells Alexis the attorneys at her office assigned to Montoya's cases never discussed them because they never make it to trial.

"His cases were always dismissed due to lack of evidence and forthcoming witnesses," Catherine explains.

"Alvin would talk about the lack of evidence to retain Montoya as well, but that's all I know Alexis." Alexis kneels down at her mother's feet and says,

"Mom, I know you don't want to hear this, but Sherman is a dirty cop. Montoya hinted at that fact tonight." Catherine steadily shakes her head back and forth.

Alexis continues, "Dad and Sherman were the arresting officers each time for Montoya. Montoya's cases would get dismissed for lack of evidence. Montoya had to be paying Sherman to get rid of the evidence…Mom, think about it."

She explains further her theory about Sherman being a "dirty cop" and his involvement in her father's death. Alexis believes her father discovered Sherman was on Montoya's payroll and confronted him about it. Sherman killed Alvin to make sure he wasn't outed. That would explain the bruises he had that day her father died and why he was so quick to take him off of life support. After listening to Alexis's every word, Catherine asks,

"Are you sure, Alexis? Do you truly believe Sherman had something to do with your father's murder? That's a strong accusation."

"I'm sure. I just need the evidence to prove it or a confession," Alexis answers. Catherine kisses Alexis on the forehead and tells her to be careful. They hug each other for a moment, then finally settle in for the night.

The next day, Alexis is the first to arrive at the precinct. She starts snooping around for evidence to link Sherman and Montoya to her father's death. Chief Sherman comes in two hours later but doesn't stay long.

"Good morning," he tells Alexis.

She stares at him with anger and disgust. She no longer sees him as a noble officer of the law. She is reluctant to greet Chief Sherman but knows she can't cause suspicion.

"Morning, sir," Alexis says. Once Chief Sherman walks into his office, Alexis continues looking for evidence.

Thirty minutes later, Chief Sherman leaves the precinct in a hurry. He tells the desk clerk he will be back in a couple of hours. Alexis thinks it's the perfect opportunity to look around his office.

As she walks toward the office door, the desk clerk looks and smiles at Alexis. She knows Alexis and Chief Sherman are "family" and doesn't hesitate to let Alexis walk right into Chief Sherman's office. After looking around for several minutes, Alexis discovers a note on Sherman's desk calendar for that day.

The note simply says, "JM 6 After Six." It is clear Sherman is meeting Jesus Montoya at six o'clock at the After Six lounge. Alexis snaps a picture of the desk calendar note with her phone. She walks out, closing the office door behind her, and heads back to her desk. She sits there combing through all of Montoya's files for the rest of the day.

Alexis heads over to the After Six lounge once her shift is over at the precinct. She knows the front door is no longer an entrance option since being escorted out the night before. She enters the lounge, undetected, walking from the loading dock, through the kitchen, and into the bartending area. She looks around and finally sees Sherman and Montoya together. They are sitting at Montoya's private table having a drink. Before finishing their drinks, the two leave out using a nearby exit door. Alexis follows them into an alley. She can hear Montoya and Sherman discussing her. She squats down nearby, takes out her cell phone, and starts to record the conversation for evidence. Montoya tells Sherman Alexis stopped by his club yesterday to have a conversation about her father's murder. Sherman asks Montoya,

"Did you tell her anything?"

"No," Montoya says,

"I did not tell her you killed her father for me." Alexis gasps. Sherman looks around and tells Montoya to keep it down, but Montoya laughs in confidence that the two are alone. Suddenly, Alexis's phone slides out of her nervous, sweaty hands and drops to the ground. Montoya and Sherman turn in her direction and sees her. Alexis takes off running, but Montoya and Sherman are right behind her.

She makes it back to her car and speeds off. As she travels few blocks down the road, she thinks she has escaped, but Montoya and Sherman are right behind her. A chase begins.

After running multiple red lights, the chase comes to an abrupt end when Alexis swerves into a pole, trying to avoid hitting a pedestrian crossing the street. Alive, but in and out of consciousness, Alexis tries reaching for her gun. She knows Montoya and Sherman are coming for her. Their car pulls up next to hers. Sherman gets out and runs up to the driver's side of Alexis's car. He drags Alexis out of the car, throws her to the ground, and viciously starts to kick her. He then pulls out his gun and jams it into the back of Alexis's head.

Just as Sherman is about to pull the trigger, Maria and Mario come to Alexis's rescue. They saw the car chase while driving down the street and followed once they realized it was Alexis. Mario fires a shot into Sherman's leg. He falls to the ground in pain.

Montoya, still in the car, tries to drive off, but Maria hits and pins his car with hers. Alexis, thinking Sherman cannot escape with a gunshot wound to the leg, gets up and heads over to the car Montoya is in. Montoya fumbles out the car and leans against it to gain balance.

Alexis looks at Montoya and asks,

"Who killed my father?"

Montoya spits at Alexis saying, "I'm not telling you shit."

Alexis punches Montoya in the face, causing him to go unconscious. She turns around to find Sherman is nowhere in sight. He's escaped. Alexis calls for backup and minutes later, police cars and EMTs pull up. As Alexis gets ready to recount the events of the evening, her phone rings. Thinking her mother, Catherine, is on the other end, she answers, but it isn't her mom. It's Sherman. He has taken Alexis's mother hostage. Sherman threatens to kill Catherine if Alexis speaks to anyone about what she has learned.

"I am going to kill her if you open your mouth," he says.

"Where are you?" Alexis asks. Sherman tells Alexis he's at her house, waiting comfortably in her father's recliner for her return home. He gives Alexis thirty minutes to get there. In the background, Alexis hears her mother saying, "Don't come. Stay away."

Before hanging up, Alexis says, "You took my father away from me. You're not taking my mother. I am coming to get you."

Sherman responds with, "Don't keep me waiting," and hangs up the phone.

Alexis pulls up at her mother's home with her gun drawn. As she walks into the kitchen, she sees her mom is on her knees, and Sherman has his gun against her head.

Sherman says, "Put the gun down and hand over the phone!"

"Let my mother go first," Alexis says.

Sherman cocks his gun and tells Alexis again to hand over her cell phone.

"Okay, stop," Alexis says, "I will give you the phone."

Alexis places her gun on a nearby bar stool. She takes her phone out of her pocket and slides it across the kitchen floor. Sherman looks at Catherine and pushes her to the ground. Catherine shuffles across the floor over to Alexis. Alexis tells her to get behind her. As Sherman lowers his gun, he says to the two of them,

"I'm sorry. I never meant for this to happen." He looks at Alexis and continues,

"Your dad was like a brother to me."

"Then why did you kill him?" Alexis asks.

"Money. The money was too great of an opportunity to turn down," Sherman says.

"So, you took my dad's life so you could get paid," Alexis says. Sherman explains to Alexis he tried to convince Alvin to join in the game, but he was too much of a boy scout. Before Alexis can respond or even make a move, she hears a gunshot, and then she sees Sherman falling to the ground. He lies lifeless on the kitchen floor with a gunshot wound right between his eyes. Catherine has crawled into the den, retrieved her gun from her purse, and shot Sherman. Catherine calmly puts down the gun and says,

"You son of a bitch. That's what you get for killing my husband."

Alexis takes the gun out of her mother's hand and hugs her. Alexis and Catherine walk out of the house, surrounded by police officers. They are placed in a police car and taken to the precinct to give formal statements.

Upon their arrival, they are greeted by Police Commissioner Jackson Clark. Commissioner Clark hugs both Alexis and Catherine.

"Congratulations on solving your father's murder," he says.

"I knew your father. He was a good cop and an even better man. My only regret is that it took six years to find the person responsible. I still can't believe James Sherman would do something like this. Now, we have to go back and look at every arrest he's ever made knowing that he was tampering with evidence."

"Thank you. I never thought Chief Sherman, I mean James Sherman, would hurt my father. They were such good friends," Alexis says.

"You are a strong young woman and an asset to this department. If you ever need anything, don't hesitate to ask," Clark says.

Alexis and Catherine leave the police precinct, elated that Alvin's murder is finally solved.

The next morning, Alexis and Catherine decide to visit Alvin's grave and place fresh flowers there.

"Baby, I miss you so much," Catherine says.

"Words can't describe how I feel. I lost my best friend and soul mate. I will always love you. You can rest easy now. Alexis and I are fine." Alexis steps up to the grave and says,

"Daddy, I miss you. I hope I've made you proud. These last six years have been hard without you, but I've taken the life lessons you taught me and moved on with my life even though not having your guidance hurts every day. Rest easy. I love you."

Alexis and Catherine gaze upon Alvin's grave for a few more minutes before heading back to the car. As they're walking, Alexis's phone suddenly rings. It is Police Commissioner Clark.

"Alexis, I am calling to let you know Jesus Montoya has escaped police custody."

Alexis replies, "What? Do you know where he's heading?"

Commissioner Clark explains he has no intel as of yet on the whereabouts of Jesus Montoya but believes Alexis and her mother may be targets if he is vengeful. As a precaution, Commissioner Clark tells the two he will have officers surveilling their home until Montoya is back in custody.

"What can I do to help?" asks Alexis.

"You've done enough solving your father's murder. We'll take it from here. But if Montoya contacts you, let us know immediately," Commissioner Clark answers.

"Yes, sir," Alexis says.

Alexis and Catherine get into the car. On their way home, Alexis fills in Catherine about Montoya escaping police custody.

"Oh my goodness. Could he be coming for us?" Catherine asks.

Alexis explains there is no reason for him to come after the two of them. The surveillance is just a precaution.

"We have nothing that he wants. If anything, he's going to try and leave town. Commissioner Clark has sidelined me and asked that I stay out of it. But I can't do that," Alexis says.

"What are you going to do?" Catherine asks.

"I'm going to drive down to his club After Six to see if he is there or if any knows his whereabouts," Alexis says.

"Okay, but, baby, be careful," Catherine says.

"I will," Alexis says.

Alexis pulls into the driveway of her home. It is lucky for Alexis they arrive before the police surveillance. She does not want anyone to stop her. She tells her mother she will call her on her way back.

Catherine gives Alexis a hug and heads into the house. Once Alexis sees her mother is safe inside their home, she pulls out of the driveway and heads to After Six.

Alexis reaches the club; she sees the security guard on duty is the same one from the other day. She walks up and asks,

"Has your boss been by tonight?"

"No. He's not here. How could he be when he's in jail? In fact, the word on the street is, you put him there," the security guard says.

"The streets are right. I did put him there, but now he's escaped and on the run. So now I have to do it again," Alexis says.

The security guard looks down at Alexis and says, "Well, I hope you don't catch him. He may not be the best guy, but this job pays the bills. There aren't a lot of jobs for an ex-con, especially one that pays this well."

Alexis responds by saying, "If you know something and don't say something, that's aiding and abetting, and that is against the law."

After standing still for a moment, the security guard finally steps to the side and says, "Well, I don't know where he is. Feel free to go in, walk around, and see for yourself."

"Thank you," Alexis says as she walks past him and into the lounge. Once she enters the lounge, Alexis heads toward the bar. She signals for the bartender.

"What can I do for you?" the bartender says.

Alexis flashes her badge and says, "I'm looking for your boss."

"I haven't seen him in a couple of days. I heard he got busted," the bartender says.

"He did, but he's escaped, and I am trying to find him," Alexis replies. The bartender tells Alexis he has no idea where Montoya is or where he could be. He explains to Alexis that he hasn't been working at After Six for very long. He is a recent hire.

After the bartender finishes his statement, Alexis slides her card over to him, asking him to give her a call if he hears or sees anything.

"You will be doing the right thing," Alexis says. The bartender nods in agreement and slides Alexis's card into his back pocket. Before leaving the bar area, Alexis asks one more question.

"Before I go, does Montoya have any family, close friends, maybe a girlfriend?" she says. The bartender looks up at Alexis and then at the stairwell.

"His girlfriend's name is Monique Hayward. Take the stairs and then a left. She should be in the office," the bartender answers.

"Thank you," Alexis says as she walks off and heads upstairs to meet Monique Hayward. Once upstairs, Alexis takes a left just like the bartender says and sees the office door. Before she can knock, she hears a voice telling her to come in.

"The door is open. Come in," says Monique. Alexis opens the door and sees Monique sitting at the desk.

"Who are you and how can I help you this evening?" Monique says.

Alexis flashes her badge and says, "My name is Alexis Sheppard. I'm APD. I have a couple of questions I need to ask you."

"Well, have a seat, officer. I may or may not have answers for you," Monique says.

Alexis begins, "Jesus Montoya, your boyfriend, escaped police custody. Has he tried to contact you?"

"No," Monique answers.

"When was the last time you two spoke to one another?" Alexis asks.

"I haven't heard from him since he used his one phone call to tell me he was arrested. He told me to call our lawyer because he was in trouble. I wanted to go down and see him, but he wanted me to stay out here and make sure the club kept running until he returns," answers Monique.

Alexis can tell Monique is withholding information. She continues asking Monique question after question, but Monique isn't folding.

"Is there someplace else he would go, a safe house of some sort?" Alexis asks.

"I can't think of any place like that, and even if I did, I wouldn't tell you. You will just kill him like you did James Sherman," Monique says.

Alexis is stunned at Monique's words. She finally stands up, looks Monique directly in the eye and says, "Your boyfriend is a dangerous criminal, and I will find him with or without your help."

Alexis heads out the door but suddenly stops and turns back toward Monique.

"I've read his past charges. There's a lot of domestic disputes between the two of you. How can you protect a man who puts his hands on you?" Alexis asks.

"I love him, and he loves me," Monique answers.

"We have a great life together." Alexis reaches for Monique's wrists and turns them over.

"It can't be that great if he leaves you with bruises and black eyes," Alexis says. Monique demands Alexis leave the office, and she does.

Alexis walks out the office and out of lounge. As Alexis walks toward her car, she notices a guy leaning on the trunk of it. She continues walking to her car, proceeding with caution. The man sees Alexis and stands straight up.

"I heard your looking for Montoya," he says.

Suspicious but determined to capture Montoya, Alexis tells the stranger yes. His name is Sam Jones, a former waiter at After Six. Montoya fired him after catching him flirting with his girlfriend, Monique. Sam tells Alexis that before he was fired, he overheard Montoya and Monique discussing an abandoned building over in the West End area, referring to it as their little "hideaway." Sam isn't able to give Alexis an exact address but tells Alexis Monique used to complain about the noise. She hated the squeals of the trains.

With all the information Sam gives Alexis, she knows where her next stop is. She tells Sam "thank you" and heads over to the West End, near the Marta station. On her way to the West End, an alert comes through the police scanner. A black SUV has been reported stolen in the exact area. Alexis wonders if it is connected to Montoya's escape.

She turns on to the street of the Marta station, driving slowly down the street. She looks for anything outside of the ordinary. Two blocks later, Alexis comes to a building with a black Ford Explorer parked in front. She turns off her headlights and parks a couple of feet away from the building. She gets out of the car, pulls out her weapon, and starts walking toward the building. She looks at the license plate on the vehicle and it matches the vehicle the police scanner reported earlier.

She turns toward the building, as sees the door is open. The lock has been broken. Alexis slowly pushes the door open and searches the bottom floor of the abandoned building but finds nothing and no one.

She walks toward the stairwell and starts hearing faint voices coming from above. Slowly, she makes her way up the stairs, making sure she is not heard. When she reaches the top of the stairwell, she sees a light coming from one of the rooms. Alexis walks toward the room's door and hears sobbing. She peers through the crack of the door and sees a young boy attempting to assault a woman.

Alexis kicks down the door and bursts into the room.

"Atlanta PD. Freeze," Alexis shouts.

"Put your hands in the air where I can see them." The young man, startled, puts his hands up.

Alexis looks down at the woman and asks if she's okay. The woman, now with tears of joy for being saved, tells Alexis "thank you."

Alexis cuffs the man and calls for backup. Once the police arrive, they take the young man into custody, and the woman is sent to the hospital in an ambulance. As crime scene investigators finish combing the area in and around the building, including the car, Alexis receives a phone call from Commissioner Clark.

"Good work, Sheppard, but I thought I told you to lay low until Montoya is back in custody," Commissioner Clark says.

"I know, but I had to do something. I can't just sit at home and do nothing. Are there any new leads on where Montoya could be?" Alexis questions.

Commissioner Clark tells Alexis although there still aren't any leads, every available unit is out there looking for Montoya. He ensures Alexis that he will keep her posted as soon as there is something. Finally, Commissioner Clark orders Alexis to go home. To show his seriousness, he has an officer trail her home. When Alexis arrives home, Catherine greets her at the door with a hug.

"Did you find him?" Catherine asks.

Alexis tells her she had no luck in finding Montoya.

"I went down to Montoya's club and questioned a couple of his employees. The bouncer, bartender, and his girlfriend, Monique Hayward. They all said they haven't heard from him and don't know where he is," Alexis says.

Catherine reassures Alexis that Montoya will be captured and adds that she will feel a lot safer when that "animal" is finally behind bars.

Catherine heads upstairs for bed. Alexis follows soon after. Around one o'clock, Alexis's cell phone rings. It's Maria.

"Alexis! You have to help us," she says.

Alexis sits up in bed.

"What's wrong?" asks Alexis.

"He says he's going to kill us," Maria answers.

Then a familiar voice is heard on the other end of the phone.

It's Montoya.

"Meet me at Piedmont Park in an hour," Montoya demands.

Before the call ends, Alexis hears Maria cry out, "please hurry."

Alexis gets dressed, grabs her badge and gun, and runs out the door. On her way, she calls Commissioner Clark and tells him about the phone call she received from her friend Maria and Montoya.

"Alexis, where are you now?" asks Commissioner Clark.

"I'm heading to the location, sir," Alexis says.

"No, wait for backup," says Clark.

"I can't, sir. He's going to kill them if I don't show up right away." Alexis hangs up the phone and speeds down to Piedmont Park.

As Alexis takes the I-75 exit to meet Montoya at Piedmont Park, she sees police lights flashing near the location of Montoya's club. She turns the volume up on her police scanner and hears, "Attention all units. Please be advised of a death scene at night club After Six." Alexis radios into dispatch for more information. The dispatcher tells Alexis an African American male, between the age of thirty and forty was shot multiple times in the parking lot of After Six.

"Witnesses at the scene say the body is Sam Jones's, a former employee at the night club," the dispatcher says.

Alexis wonders if it is the man who approached her earlier today with information regarding Montoya's whereabouts. She searches the name Sam Jones in the MDT. She is right. The victim, Sam Jones, is indeed the man who helped her earlier. Alexis knows she has to hurry to save Maria and Mario.

The clock on the dashboard reads 2:00 am. A normal thirty-minute drive to Piedmont Park only took fifteen minutes for Alexis. As she pulls into the park's entrance, she sees the gleaming taillights of a black sedan.

Suddenly, the trunk pops open. A tall, dark-haired man exits the vehicle, but it isn't Montoya. It is the bodyguard from Montoya's club, After Six. He walks to the trunk and opens it up all the way. Alexis watches as the bodyguard pulls Maria out and onto the ground by her hair. Maria is sobbing hysterically.

The bodyguard reaches into the trunk again and pulls Mario out. He is badly beaten. Alexis knows she has to act fast. Before exiting her vehicle, Alexis reloads the rounds of her gun. She jumps out ready to save her friend Maria, but more ready to catch Montoya. Instantaneously, Alexis hears multiple gunshots followed by horrified screams from Maria. In the second it took Alexis to get out of her car, Montoya's bodyguard fired two shots into Mario's head, and now Mario's body lies lifeless at Maria's feet.

"Querida," says a voice all too familiar to Alexis. It is Montoya, stepping out from the back seat of the sedan. He walks up to Maria and says to her, "Don't cry. I just did you a favor. I got rid of a rat." Montoya and his bodyguard begin to laugh. Maria tries to lunge toward Montoya, but his bodyguard grabs her.

"Feisty," says Montoya. Before Montoya can say or do anything else, Alexis swiftly walks up.

"Freeze, Montoya! It's over!" Alexis shouts.

"It's not over. Well, not yet" Montoya says.

"I need my money," he continues.

"What money?" questions Alexis.

A faint grin surfaces upon Montoya's face. Slowly, he starts walking toward Alexis but stops after hearing the click of her gun's safety.

"Alexis, I should have been more honest with you the other day at my club," Montoya says.

"What do you mean 'more honest'?" questions Alexis.

"Did you have something to do with my father's death? Did you kill my father?" It's evident in Alexis's voice and body language that her anger is growing. Montoya stares at Alexis with joy, knowing he is getting under her skin.

"No, I didn't kill him, sweetheart. Your dad was a very valuable asset to me. He also stole five million dollars from me, to be exact."

"I told you your dad was one of the good cops, but I knew differently." Montoya takes a small step toward Alexis.

"Stay back!" Alexis demands.

"What are you saying to me about my father?" With his grin wider than before, Montoya continues.

"Alvin Sheppard, the slain APD officer, wasn't the boy scout everyone proclaimed him to be."

"Your father was on my payroll, just like Sherman." Montoya pauses to study Alexis's reaction to his words. Her eyes read of disbelief. Thoughts are running wildly in her head. She doesn't know what to say or do, but she tries to stay focused, keeping her gun steady and pointed at Montoya. Finally, Alexis says, "You're lying. My father would never work for anyone like you!"

"No, you wish I was lying, but I'm telling the truth," Montoya responds.

"Your dad was so dirty he even stole from me, but no one steals from me and lives." With the drop of his chin, Montoya's voice deepens as he continues his conversation with Alexis.

"And I always get back what was taken from me. I want my five million dollars, Alexis. I want my money back, and you're going to get it for me."

"I don't know where your money is, and even if I did, what makes you think I'm going to give it to you?" Alexis says.

Montoya snaps his fingers. The goon restraining Maria pulls out a gun and points it directly into Maria's temporal.

"If you don't give me my money, she dies," Montoya answers.

Alexis screams, "Stop! Stop! I don't know where your money is, and my father was not a criminal." Montoya snaps his fingers again. The bodyguard throws Maria up against the car.

Alexis says, "Stop! Don't hurt her!"

"Do you know where your father hid my money?" Montoya asks.

"No, I have no idea," says Alexis.

"Well, you better find it. You have until dawn to get me my money. If you don't, your friend dies," Montoya says.

He walks up closer to Alexis and hands her a cell phone. He tells Alexis to call him once she has the money. From there, he will give her the location to hand off the money for Maria.

Alexis gets back into her car and drives back home. Once Alexis arrives home, she bursts through the door, yelling for her mother. Catherine comes running downstairs asking Alexis what's wrong. Alexis tells Catherine everything from Maria's phone call to Mario's murder, and Montoya's demand of five million dollars. She even tells Catherine about Montoya calling her father a "dirty cop." Catherine sits back in disbelief. Her eyes start welling up with tears as she struggles to find the words to speak. Catherine turns to Alexis and says, "Your father was the best man I've ever met. There is absolutely no way he would ever do what that animal said he did."

Alexis grabs her mother's hand.

"Mom, I don't want to believe it either, but Montoya was pretty convincing. He is positive that dad stole five million dollars from him," Alexis says. Alexis looks down at her watch.

"Mom, if I don't have the money in the next three hours, he is going to kill Maria. He's already killed Maria's boyfriend, Mario," Alexis says.

"I know this is difficult, and I know you don't want to believe it, but is there any place dad could have hidden the money in this house and you do not know about it?"

Catherine stands up and starts pacing back and forth, thinking of any possible place the money could be hidden. She suddenly stops and says,

"Your dad was spending a lot of time in the basement right before his death. I would ask him what he was doing down there. He would get very dismissive, telling me he's cleaning his gun collection. I didn't think anything else of it. But his gun collection used to be in the attic, then out of nowhere, he moved them to the basement. I haven't been down in the basement since your father's funeral."

Alexis tells her mom they need to check out the basement, and the two begin walking toward the door leading to it. Catherine is right behind her. Alexis opens the door, turns on her flashlight, and starts walking down the steps. Catherine tells Alexis to wait; she knows where the light switch is. Once the lights are on, Catherine and Alexis continue walking down the steps until they reach the bottom. There, Alexis tries to think as her father would and starts searching for possible places the money could be. She looks behind an old bookshelf and finds nothing.

Catherine asks, "Alexis, what should we be looking for?"

"You're looking for anything out of the ordinary. Something that looks out of place," Alexis says.

They continue searching for another ten minutes when Catherine notices a purple rug near Alvin's gun collection. The rug hasn't always been there; it's the only thing out of the ordinary. Alexis walks over to the rug and sees her dad's tool chest sitting on top of the rug. She asks her mom to help her move the chest off the rug.

Once the tool chest is removed, Alexis pulls back the rug and notices that there is a door with a combination lock on it. Alexis asks her mother if she has any idea what the combination could be. Catherine says no, so they start trying different combinations. She tries her mom's birthday first, 8/15/69. It doesn't work. She then tries her mom and dad's anniversary, 6/25/91. No luck.

Finally, Alexis tries her birthday, 3/7/96, and it works. She opens the door, and there's a ladder. Alexis turns on her flashlight and begins to climb down the ladder.

"Be careful," Catherine says.

Alexis gets to the bottom of the ladder. She sees a light switch on the wall and turns on the light. There's an old refrigerator in the corner. She walks toward the refrigerator and opens the door. Alexis is stunned at the sight of five million dollars. Alexis screams, "Mom, I found it. It looks like the money Montoya has been looking for."

"I need to see it for myself," Catherine says and climbs down the ladder. Staring in disbelief, she says, "Oh, Alvin, how could you?"

Alexis looks down at her watch and says, "Mom, I only have three hours to get this money to Montoya. Can you find one of dad's old duffle bags. I need something to put the money in." Catherine climbs back up the ladder and goes back upstairs. She looks in her bedroom's closet and finds two duffle bags. She hurries back down to the basement where Alexis is waiting. The two women begin counting and putting the money into the bags. When they are done, Alexis checks her watch again and sees she has two and a half hours left. She reaches into her pocket and pulls out the phone Montoya gave her. She dials the only number programmed into the phone. After a couple of quick rings, Montoya answers in an angry voice.

"Do you have my money?" he asks.

"Yes, but first let me talk to Maria. I want to make sure she's okay," Alexis says.

Montoya agrees but tells Alexis to make it quick.

"Maria? Are you okay? Have they hurt you?" Alexis asks.

"I'm okay, for now. They haven't hurt me but, Lexi, hurry. I'm scared," Maria says, crying.

"Don't worry, I'm on my way," Alexis says.

Montoya grabs the phone from Maria and tells Alexis to meet him at the Fulton County Airport–Brown Field by 5:00 am. Alexis agrees and hangs up the phone. Alexis shares a hug with her mother, Catherine. She then heads up the ladder and out of the door with the money. She jumps in her car and heads toward the airport.

On the way, she calls Commissioner Clark and brings him up to speed since their last conversation. Alexis tells Commissioner Clark that Montoya has kidnapped her friend Maria, killed Maria's boyfriend Mario, and that he wants her to meet him at Fulton County Airport at 5:00 am. Commissioner Clark tells Alexis he's sending units to the airport for backup.

"Wait for backup," Commissioner Clark says.

"Sorry, sir, I can't wait. If I do that, he might kill Maria. I can't let that happen," Alexis says.

"Understood, just be careful," Clark responds.

Alexis races toward the airport. She gets there ten minutes to five. Suddenly, the phone rings and it's Montoya. He tells her to meet him at the hangar at the end of the runway. Alexis says okay. She drives down to the hangar, gets out of the car, and starts walking to the doors of the hangar. The doors begin to open. She sees Montoya holding a gun to Maria's head.

"Toss me my money," Montoya says.

"Let her go first," Alexis demands.

"I'm not playing games with you. Toss me my money," Montoya says.

"No! Not until you let her go," Alexis says.

Slowly, Montoya releases his grip of Maria, and she walks toward Alexis. Alexis tosses the duffle bags in Montoya's direction. Maria runs to Alexis and gives her a hug. Alexis tells Maria to get behind her. She pulls her gun out and tells Montoya he's under arrest for the murders of Alvin Sheppard and Mario Espinoza. Montoya laughs.

"I've been one step ahead of you the whole time," he says.

Suddenly, Montoya's bodyguard and girlfriend walk up behind Alexis and Maria with their guns drawn at them. Alexis drops her gun, realizing she's outnumbered. Montoya tells his bodyguard to tie up Alexis and Maria. There's a struggle, but the bodyguard is able to tie the two up and toss them into a corner. Montoya begins to tell Alexis how he plans to leave the country and go home to Mexico.

"It's a shame your father was murdered. He was one of my best employees," Montoya says.

"I'm going to take this money and start over in Mexico."

Alexis says, "I still don't believe my dad had a part in this, but believe this, there is no place you can go where I won't find you."

Montoya begins to laugh.

"I'd like to see you try. After I leave Atlanta, you will never see me again," Montoya says. Montoya receives a phone call from his pilot. The plane is gassed up and ready to go.

"Goodbye, Miss Sheppard. I hope we never meet again," Montoya says.

"I have a knife in my pocket. I think I can reach it," Maria says.

The two women struggle for a second, but eventually Maria is able to slide the knife from her pocket. She slides the knife over to Alexis, and she begins cutting the rope that is restraining them. Alexis finally manages to break free. She looks around the hangar for a weapon. She finds the biggest torque wrench she could find. Alexis and Maria walk up and see Montoya's bodyguard standing at the bottom steps of the airplane. His back is turned. Alexis tells Maria to stay put. She creeps up slowly behind the bodyguard and hits him upside the head with the wrench. The bodyguard falls to the ground unconscious.

Alexis takes his gun. She looks over at Maria and waves for her to come join her. Alexis and Maria slowly walk up the steps to the plane. They see Montoya and his girlfriend, Monique, preparing to eat dinner. Suddenly, the plane's engines start up.

Alexis points her gun at Montoya and says, "I told you. You will not get away from me."

Montoya reaches for his gun, but before he can get it, Alexis shoots him in the chest. Montoya falls to the floor dead. Monique, angry and distraught, charges toward Alexis. Alexis pistol whips Monique, and she falls to the floor. Alexis runs to the cockpit and tells the pilot to shut off the engines. She walks the pilot out of the door and down the steps. She ties him to the stairwell. She goes back into the plane and looks over to where Maria is hiding behind a seat. She tells her it's safe to come out. The two women share a hug. Alexis walks over to the two bags of money, grabs each, and walks off the plane.

"I'm glad that's over," Maria says.

"Me too," Alexis says.

Ten minutes later, Commissioner Clark and officers arrive at the scene. Commissioner Clark gets out of the car and shakes Alexis's hand.

"Damn good work, Sheppard. Your father would be proud of you. If there is ever anything you need, don't hesitate to reach out," Commissioner Clark says.

"Thank you, sir. I could use a couple of days off," Alexis says.

Commissioner Clark chuckles, "I think you've earned some time off. I will see you in two weeks."

Alexis tells him "thank you." She then gets on the phone with her mom.

"Mom, it's over. I got him," Alexis says.

Catherine says, "Are you okay, baby? Are you hurt?"

"No. I'm fine, Mom. I'm on my way home," Alexis says.

END